To Ben, my pants-tastic illustrator ~ C. F.

For Matilda, with love ~ B. C.

ALADDIN

An imprint of Simon & Schuster Children's Publishing Division

1230 Avenue of the Americas, New York, NY 10020

First Aladdin hardcover edition March 2012

Text copyright © 2009 by Claire Freedman

Illustrations copyright © 2009 by Ben Cort

For information about special discounts for bulk purchases,

please contact Simon & Schuster Special Sales at 1-866-506-1949or business@simonandschuster.com.

The Simon & Schuster Speakers Bureau can bring authors to your live event.

For more information or to book an event contact the Simon & Schuster Speakers Bureau at

1-866-248-3049 or visit our website at www.simonspeakers.com.

The text of this book was set in Plumbsky Black.

Manufactured in China 0316 SUK

4 6 8 10 9 7 5 3

This book has been cataloged with the Library of Congress.

ISBN 978-1-4424-2768-6

ISBN 978-1-4424-4097-5 (eBook)

Aliens in Underpants Save the World

ILLUSTRATED BY
Ben Cort

CLAIRE FREEDMAN

aladdin

NEW YORK   LONDON   TORONTO   SYDNEY   NEW DELHI

Aliens love underpants.

It's lucky that they do.

For underpants saved our universe.

Sounds crazy, but it's true!

On one pants-pinching mission,
the aliens zoomed through space.
The spaceships shook and wobbled.
Their hearts began to race.

Their radars bleeped, their sirens wailed,
on came the warning light!
Heading straight for planet Earth
was one huge meteorite!

Meanwhile, on Earth, the scientists
had such an awful fright.
"What's THAT?" they gulped
in horror,
"Picked up on our satellite?"

The fire engines came racing,
   police and air rescue, too,
But with just four hours till impact,
   there was little they could do!

Down to Earth the aliens shot,
and they jumped out with
a shout,

"No time to lose, if Earth blows up,
our underpants supply runs out!"

They took undies down from clotheslines,
and raided all the stores.
They sneaked inside our houses
and pulled bloomers out of
drawers.

The aliens stitched the underwear,
and proudly they unfurled,
The most GINORMOUS pair of
underpants made in the whole
wide world!

Quickly with their spaceships,
 they stretched the underpants in place.
And when the meteor landed,
 it zoomed back to outer space!

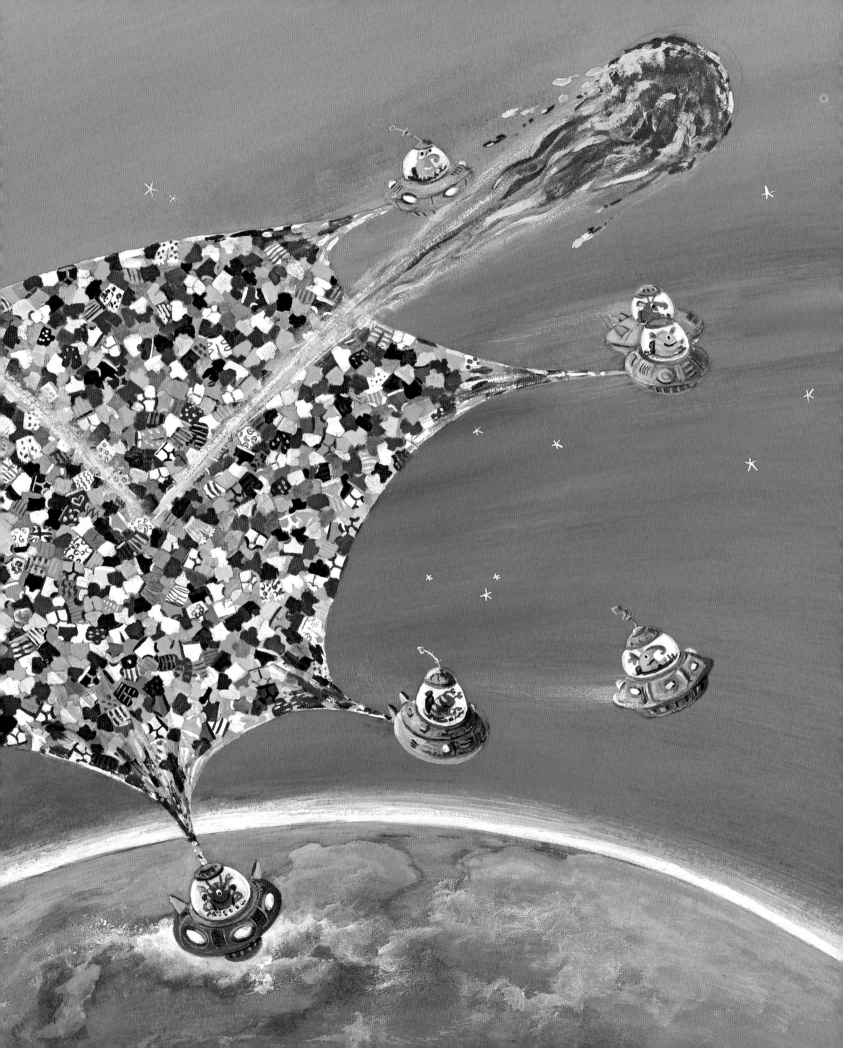

"The meteorite has vanished!"
gasped the people in surprise,
"We thought we saw huge underpants,
but can't believe our eyes!"

Back at home the aliens cheered,
"Our pants plan was fantastic!
We saved the Earth with underpants
so stretchy and elastic!"

So should your pants go missing,
  there's no need to make a fuss.
Let the aliens have their fun.
They've done SO much for us!